★ WE ARE HEROES ★

SKATEBOARD BUDDY

by Jon Mikkelsen
illustrated by Nathan Lueth

Librarian Reviewer
Marci Peschke
Librarian, Dallas Independent School District
MA Education Reading Specialist, Stephen F. Austin State University
Learning Resources Endorsement, Texas Women's University

Reading Consultant
Elizabeth Stedem
Educator/Consultant, Colorado Springs, CO
MA in Elementary Education, University of Denver, CO

STONE ARCH BOOKS
www.stonearchbooks.com

Keystone Books are published by Stone Arch Books
151 Good Counsel Drive, P.O. Box 669
Mankato, Minnesota 56002
www.stonearchbooks.com

Library of Congress Cataloging-in-Publication Data
Mikkelsen, Jon.
    Skateboard Buddy / by Jon Mikkelsen; illustrated by Nathan Lueth.
    p. cm. — (Keystone Books. We Are Heroes)
    ISBN 978-1-4342-0788-3 (library binding)
    ISBN 978-1-4342-0884-2 (pbk.)
    [1. Mentoring—Fiction.] I. Lueth, Nathan, ill. II. Title.
PZ7.M5926Sk 2009
[Fic]—dc22   2008008121

Summary: Jason has to help a younger kid learn about science. Is there
any way to make it fun?

Art Director: Heather Kindseth
Graphic Design: Brann Garvey

1 2 3 4 5 6 13 12 11 10 09 08

Printed in the United States of America

TABLE OF CONTENTS

Jason had not been looking forward to Tuesday. Tuesday was Volunteer Day in Mr. White's class.

"I don't need to learn about volunteering," Jason told his friend Milo. "I'm going to be too busy being a famous basketball star, making lots of money, and being really rich."

Mr. White heard what Jason said. The teacher walked over to Jason.

"Being rich isn't everything," said Mr. White. "In fact, many rich people, including basketball stars, spend lots of time volunteering."

Jason didn't like the sound of volunteering. It could take time away from his main passion, basketball.

"I'll volunteer after I'm a basketball star," he joked to Milo.

"Before you do that, you better work on your lay-ups," Milo shot back.

"To give you all a better idea of volunteering, you are each going to be mentoring," said Mr. White.

"What's mentoring?" asked Milo.

"A mentor is someone who helps out and teaches someone with less experience," said Mr. White.

"Like a teacher?" asked Jason. "I don't want to be a teacher. I just want to play basketball!"

"Sort of like a teacher," Mr. White said. "But the main thing is helping someone who needs it. Next week, the entire class will go to the Youth Center. You will each be assigned someone to mentor."

"But next week is the big game against the Lawton Lions!" complained Jason. "What if we're not back in time for practice?"

Mr. White sighed. "You will be back in time," he said. "And sometimes there are more important things than basketball."

Jason frowned and said, "I'll pretend I didn't hear that."

Chapter 2

At the Youth Center the next week, each student was given a different adult supervisor to help them during the mentoring program.

Jason's supervisor was a woman named Ms. Krauss. He went into her office and sat down. After a few minutes, Ms. Krauss came in with a boy who looked like he was about eight years old. He was carrying a skateboard.

"Jason, this is Ben," said Ms. Krauss, "Ben, this is Jason. He's the mentor I was telling you about."

Ben didn't even look up from the floor.

"Hey," said Jason.

"Hey," said Ben.

Great, thought Jason. *This kid is as bored as I am. Mentoring is not exciting.*

Ben sat down in the chair next to Jason. His skateboard fell to the floor at his feet.

"Ben, Jason was chosen to be your mentor because he gets great grades in science," said Ms. Krauss.

"Good for him," said Ben with a sneer.

Ms. Krauss sighed. Then she said, "Jason is the best in his class."

Jason was surprised. It was true that he loved science, but he didn't know he was the best in his class. Mr. White must have told Ms. Krauss. Jason felt a little proud.

"Jason is going to help you out with your science homework this week," Ms. Krauss told Ben.

"Whatever," said Ben. He rolled his eyes.

"I'll let you guys talk," said Ms. Krauss. She stood up and walked toward the door. Then she added, "I'll be back in fifteen minutes."

The door closed. Jason looked at Ben. "Do you like science?" Jason asked.

"No," said Ben. "I'm only here because my teacher made me. Science is boring. I don't like science, and I don't like school, and I don't want anyone to help me."

"Oh," Jason said. He wasn't sure what else to say. The boys sat in silence for a long time.

Finally, Ms. Krauss came back in the room. "That's all for today," she said. "I'll see you two here tomorrow."

Jason jumped out of his chair. Then he ran from the room.

In the hallway, he nearly knocked Milo over.

"How did it go?" asked Milo.

"It was awful," said Jason. "I knew I was going to hate this mentor thing!"

Chapter 3

The next day, Jason and Ben sat in a small room at the Youth Center. They both opened their textbooks. Ben's class was learning about gravity.

"Let's start with the basics," Jason said. "What is gravity?"

"I don't know," said Ben.

"I'll help you out," said Jason. "Gravity is the force that pulls things toward the center of the earth."

"So?" said Ben. Ben stared out the window at the skate park behind the Youth Center. The sun was shining. It was a perfect fall day.

Jason sighed. He wished he were outside too.

"Maybe we can try a different way," Jason said. "How does gravity affect you?"

"It doesn't," said Ben. "It's just some stupid thing written in a book."

Jason closed his book and tried not to get mad. He knew that Ben was wrong. Jason knew that you could see science everywhere you looked. In a rainbow, in your lunch, even in sports.

That's when it hit him. "You like to skateboard, right?" asked Jason.

"Yeah," said Ben. He smiled a little. "I'm just learning, though. I'm not very good yet. I keep falling over and stuff."

"Let's go outside," Jason said. "If you understand gravity, you'll be a better skateboarder."

"Whatever," said Ben. "I have nothing better to do."

Jason knew he could change Ben's mind.

Chapter 4

SCIENCE AND SKATEBOARDS

Jason told Ms. Krauss his plan. Then he and Ben went outside.

There was a skate park behind the Youth Center. It had tons of iron railings and concrete blocks to skate on. It even had a small half-pipe.

Jason headed straight for the half-pipe. Ben followed him.

"Why are we here?" asked Ben.

Ben looked around. Then he added, "How is this supposed to help me in science?"

"We use science all the time in our everyday lives," said Jason. "You just have to know where to look. What do you think gravity has to do with skateboarding?"

Ben rolled his eyes. "Even I know that," he said. "If you mess up, you crash. That's gravity."

"That's part of it," said Jason, "but there's way more."

Jason picked up two rocks. One of the rocks was about the size of his palm. The other rock was much smaller. It wasn't much bigger than a pebble.

"If I drop these at the same time, which do you think will hit the ground first?" Jason asked.

Ben looked at the rocks. Then he said, "The bigger one will hit the ground first because it weighs more."

"Are you sure about that?" asked Jason.

Ben looked at Jason and frowned. "Of course I'm sure," he said.

Jason dropped the rocks. They both hit the ground at the same time.

Ben's eyes got wide. He looked shocked. "How did you do that?" he asked.

"I didn't do anything," Jason said. "That's gravity. It doesn't matter how much something weighs. If you drop two things from the same height, they fall at the same speed. It doesn't matter if one is way bigger than the other. Isn't that cool?"

Then Jason took Ben's skateboard. "I have something else to show you," Jason said.

Jason stood on the skateboard at one end of the half-pipe. He carefully balanced himself.

He looked at Ben and asked, "What do you think will happen when I step off the edge and roll down the slope of the half-pipe?"

Ben laughed.

"That's easy," Ben said. "You'll roll down, and then start rolling up the other side. If you go fast enough, you might even go into the air on the far side."

"That's right," said Jason. "What would happen if I lost control of the board and started falling? What do you think would hit the ground first, me or the board?"

Ben frowned. "You'll both hit the ground at the same time!" he said.

Jason pushed off the edge of the half-pipe. He sped down and went up the other side. He flew up into the air.

While he was in the air, he pulled his feet away from the board. He knew he was going to crash to the ground.

Ben could see that both Jason and the board fell at the same speed. They hit the ground at the same time.

"Oof!" said Jason as he landed.

Ben rushed over to help him. "Are you all right?" he asked.

Jason smiled. "I'm fine," he said. "I just wanted to show you that you can see science in all kinds of things we do every day. Plus, when you know some stuff about science, you'll get even better at skateboarding!"

"How will that make me better?" Ben asked.

"Well," Jason replied, "when you know what's going on under your feet, you'll be better at it. Trust me."

"I want to try!" said Ben.

He grabbed the board. Then he ran to the top of the half-pipe.

"Don't do what I did," said Jason. "Stay on the board."

"I will," said Ben. Then he took off down the half-pipe.

After a couple of hours, it was dark out. "I better get going," said Ben. He had a smile on his face. "Thanks for everything!"

"Sure," said Jason.

Ben ran off. Jason smiled to himself.

Chapter 5

A few days later, Jason was in Mr. White's class. There were a few minutes before the bell rang, and Jason was finishing his report on the mentor program.

Milo leaned over from his desk. "What are you doing?" he asked. "I thought you hated the mentor thing. But you're writing your report like a madman! It must have been good."

Jason shrugged. "It was better than I thought," he said. "I actually had a good time. We went skateboarding."

"Cool!" said Milo.

"What did you do?" Jason asked.

Milo sighed. "We studied the life cycle of the earthworm at the library," he said. "For six hours."

"I'll collect the reports now," said Mr. White.

Jason handed his report to Mr. White. Mr. White smiled at him and asked, "So, what did you think? Was it that bad to be a mentor?"

Jason rubbed his shoulder, where he'd hurt himself when he fell from the skateboard. "It wasn't bad," he said. "I still want to be a famous basketball player. But being a mentor was okay. And helping someone else was pretty fun."

"I think you got the point," said Mr. White. "It seems like you changed your mind about mentoring."

"Yes," said Jason. "And it only took a little gravity to help me change my mind!"

ABOUT THE AUTHOR

Jon Mikkelsen has written dozens of plays for kids, which have involved aliens, superheroes, and more aliens. He acts on stage and loves performing in front of an audience. Jon also loves sushi, cheeseburgers, and pizza. He loves to travel, and has visited Moscow, Berlin, London, and Amsterdam. He lives in Minneapolis and has a cat named Coco, who does not pay rent.

ABOUT THE ILLUSTRATOR

Nathan Lueth has been a freelance illustrator since 2004. He graduated from the Minneapolis College of Art and Design in 2004, and has done work for companies like Target, General Mills, and Wreked Records. Nathan was a 2008 finalist in Tokyopop's Rising Stars of Manga contest. He lives in Minneapolis, Minnesota.

GLOSSARY

affect (uh-FEKT)—to influence or change something or someone

basics (BAY-siks)—the most important things to know about a subject

experience (ek-SPEER-ee-uhnss)—knowledge and skill

force (FORSS)—a power acting on something else to make it do something

gravity (GRAV-uh-tee)—the force that pulls things down toward the ground and keeps them from floating away into space

mentor (MEN-tur)—someone who helps someone younger or less experienced

passion (PASH-uhn)—if something is your passion, you have great love or enthusiasm for it, or it is your favorite thing

supervisor (SOO-pur-vye-zur)—someone who watches over and directs the work of other people

volunteer (vol-uhn-TEER)—someone who does a job without pay

MORE ABOUT BEING A BUDDY

Have you ever been a buddy? Ever had one? Then you know what a powerful and positive difference a buddy can make in someone's life. If you would like to make a younger kid's life better, being a buddy is a great place to start.

When you're someone's buddy, you spend time with that person. You develop a friendship with them. You also help them with schoolwork.

Sometimes, you might talk about problems they are having at school, with friends, or at home.

Having a buddy is good for both people. The younger buddy benefits from the older student's knowledge, experience, and skill. And the older buddy gains confidence when they see that they can help someone.

Older buddies need to be dependable. Their younger buddies are going to count on them to show up when they say they will. Older buddies also need to be prepared and plan ahead.

But the meetings don't have to be boring. An older buddy can find ways to make the time spent learning and talking with their younger buddy fun and exciting.

If you want to be a buddy, talk to your teacher. If he or she can't help you, try asking your school's counselor. Many schools have buddy programs in place. And if yours doesn't, maybe you can start one!

DISCUSSION QUESTIONS

1. Would you want to be a buddy or mentor to a younger kid? Why or why not?

2. Can you think of other ways that Jason could have taught Ben about science?

3. Jason and Ben used skateboards to learn about science, but Milo and his buddy studied at the library. Which way do you think is better? Why?

WRITING PROMPTS

1. Have you ever helped someone younger than you learn something? Write about what happened.

2. Do you have any friends who are much younger than you? What is that friendship like?

3. Sometimes it's interesting to think about a story from another person's point of view. Try writing chapter 2 from Ben's point of view. What does he see and hear? What does he think about? How does he feel?

IF YOU LIKE THIS BOOK

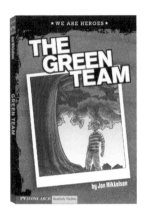

The Green Team
by Jon Mikkelsen

Noah Green decides to plant
new trees at school. He can't
do it alone. But will he be
able to convince anyone to
help him?

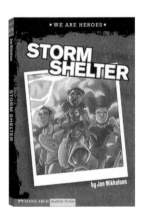

Storm Shelter
by Jon Mikkelsen

After a tornado, Nathan, Ben,
and Alison find a stray dog
stranded in a tree. The three
friends hope they'll be able
to save the lonely dog. But is
someone else out to trap the
missing mutt?

CHECK OUT...

Race for Home
by Jon Mikkelsen

Tomas sees a poster for a bike race. But he doesn't have a bike! Luckily, he meets Miles, who has an old rusty bike that they can fix up. But how can they be a team when one of them is keeping secrets?

Kids Against Hunger
by Jon Mikkelsen

It's not fair. Greg seems to skip soccer practice at least once a week. One day, Caleb and Ian follow him straight to a creepy old warehouse. What's inside? And what is Greg's big secret?

INTERNET SITES

Do you want to know more about subjects related to this book? Or are you interested in learning about other topics? Then check out FactHound, a fun, easy way to find Internet sites.

Our investigative staff has already sniffed out great sites for you!

Here's how to use FactHound:

1. Visit *www.facthound.com*

2. Select your grade level.

3. To learn more about subjects related to this book, type in the book's ISBN number: **9781434207883**.

4. Click the **Fetch It** button.

FactHound will fetch the best Internet sites for you!